Mystery Pups

DOGNAPPED!

D0200097

Also in the Mystery Pups series:

Framed!
Missing!

And, coming soon . . .

Diamond Dogs!

Mystery Pups

DOGNAPPED!

by Jodie Mellor

Illustrated by Penny Dann

SIMON AND SCHUSTER

SIMON AND SCHUSTER
First published in Great Britain in 2008 by Simon and Schuster UK Ltd
A CBS COMPANY

Text copyright © 2008 Jenny Oldfield
Illustrations copyright © 2008 Penny Dann
Cover illustration copyright © 2008 John Butler

This book is copyright under the Berne Convention.
No reproduction without permission.
All rights reserved.

The right of Jenny Oldfield to be identified as the author of this work and of Penny Dann
and John Butler to be identified as the respective interior and cover illustrators of this work
has been asserted by them in accordance with sections 77 and 78 of the Copyright,
Designs and Patents Act, 1988.

3 5 7 9 10 8 6 4

Simon & Schuster UK Ltd
1st Floor, 222 Gray's Inn Road, London WC1X 8HB

This book is a work of fiction. Names, characters, places and incidents are either the
product of the author's imagination or are used fictitiously. Any resemblance to actual
people living or dead, events or locales is entirely coincidental.

A CIP catalogue record for this book is available from the British Library.

ISBN: 978-1-84738-224-5

Printed and bound in Great Britain
by CPI Cox and Wyman, Reading, Berkshire RG1 8EX

www.simonandschuster.co.uk

CHAPTER ONE

"Hey, Caitlin – we're making badges for our new Magic Mountain Puppy Club. You can join too!" Lauren called to her friend as she came into the kitchen.

"Yes, join our club!" Megan nodded, her dark hair flopping over her face.

"But I don't have a real puppy," Caitlin said wistfully. Her toy dog was tucked under her arm. "I only have Daisy."

Megan smiled and patted the cuddly Yorkie. She knew Caitlin's parents were strict about pets. "But Daisy's so cute!"

"Here, grab these scissors," Lauren said.

"Help us make these badges!"

So Caitlin perched Daisy on the table beside the crayons and felt-tips. "Sit!" she said, laughing.

"Draw her picture," Megan ordered. "Then cut it out and give it to Lauren. She'll run it through the badge-making machine."

"Look, this is Buster!" Lauren announced proudly. She showed Caitlin her drawing of a scruffy, light-brown crossbreed pup. "Isn't he cool?"

"And this is my picture of Dylan," Megan added. "He's a black Labrador. Wait till you see him – he's so-o-o cute!" Both girls had been down to the local rescue centre to choose their very own puppies, and now they chattered about them non-stop.

"I'm making a medal thingy to hang around Buster's neck," Lauren said, rushing on to the next task.

"A medallion?" Megan asked.

"Yes, a medallion." Lauren used a gold pen. "We'll have badges and the puppies will have medallions."

"Cool," Caitlin said, busily drawing Daisy's long, silky fringe. "So, when can you bring Dylan and Buster home?"

"Tomorrow!" Megan and Lauren said together. Their eyes shone.

"Why don't you come with us?" Lauren invited Caitlin. "And bring Daisy too!"

"Be good, Daisy!" Caitlin whispered, giving her toy dog a little squeeze – *squeak-squeak*. She jumped out of the car and followed Megan and Lauren across the yard towards the Magic Mountain Rescue Centre.

Lauren's dad paused to talk with Megan's mum, while the girls ran on ahead. Lauren dashed through the door into the waiting area.

"I can't wait to see Buster!" she cried, ringing the bell on the desk.

Drrrring!

An old man with gold-rimmed glasses, white hair and a long moustache came in. He smiled at the girls and the two grown-ups. "Have you come to collect Buster and Dylan?"

"Yes, please! Are they ready?" Megan asked. It seemed ages since she and Lauren had chosen the two pups, though really it was only a couple of days.

"Absolutely." The old man's eyes twinkled as he spoke. "I've fed them and brushed their coats. They know this is their big day."

"Can we see them?" Lauren begged.

"Wait here," he said, stooping to give little Daisy a pat on the head. "Sweet," he murmured.

Caitlin smiled bravely. "Yes, but I wish she was real."

"Your mum and dad won't let you have a live one, eh?" the old man asked.

"Mum's too busy," Caitlin said sadly, letting her long hair fall across her face. "She says maybe one day…"

"One day, who knows?" Smiling, the old man went to fetch the pups.

Lauren sat on the waiting-room bench, tapping her feet impatiently.

"Calm down," her dad told her.

Megan stood by the window. "One-and-two-and-three-and—"

Caitlin frowned. "What's with the counting?"

"Four-and-five. I'm making the time go quicker. Six-and-seven…"

By the time Megan had counted to thirty, the old man was back.

"This is Dylan," he said, handing the black puppy to her. "And this is Buster – oo-ooops!"

A light-brown pup jumped from his arms and made a break for it, scampering across the room.

"Come here, Buster!" Lauren cried. She chased him under the bench.

"Yap!" he said. "Yap-yap!"

"Oh Dylan, you're so gorgeous!" Megan whispered. She cuddled her warm puppy close to her chest. She could feel his little heart beating almost as fast as her own.

The black Labrador put out his pink tongue and licked Megan's hand. He had big brown eyes and floppy ears. He wagged his little tail.

"Buster, come here!" Lauren grinned as her pup wriggled out from under the bench and charged towards her. "Good boy!" she sighed as he jumped into her arms at last.

"Keep still!" Caitlin murmured to Daisy under her breath. "Be good!"

The old man who ran the rescue centre caught Caitlin's eye and smiled kindly at her.

"Yes, one day, who knows?" he muttered to himself. Then he turned to talk to the grown-ups and asked them to fill in some forms.

Lauren held Buster tight. Untidy curls fell over her eyes. "You're even more fantastic than I remember!" she sighed. "You're perfect!"

"Keep an eye on that pup – he's into everything," the Magic Mountain man warned Lauren's dad. "A real livewire."

"A bit like his new owner!" said Lauren's dad, winking at his daughter.

Megan smiled from ear to ear as she cuddled her very own puppy. "Can we buy Dylan a red collar?" she asked her mum.

Lauren's mum nodded. "He really is lovely," she said, smiling.

"And that one is smart as can be," the old man said, pointing to Dylan. "Nothing gets past him, believe me!"

At last, the forms were signed and they were ready to leave.

The owner shook everyone by the hand.

"Thank you for coming to Magic Mountain and offering Buster and Dylan new homes," he said.

"Thank *you!*" Megan and Lauren replied eagerly.

The old man smiled and held open the door. "Take good care of them," he added, his grey eyes shining. Then he smiled at Caitlin, who was the last to leave. "These are special puppies."

She smiled back, hugging Daisy to her.

He closed the door after her. "All three of them are very special puppies indeed."

CHAPTER TWO

"Sit, Buster!" Lauren said.

The mongrel pup ignored her, running up and down Megan's long garden. He sniffed at the flowers, then rolled on the grass.

"Sit!" Megan told Dylan. "It's time to start our Magic Mountain Puppy Club." She held up his medallion, which hung from a bright-red ribbon.

Dylan wagged his tail obediently, then sat.

Caitlin put Daisy beside Dylan. Daisy's brown puppy eyes shone brightly behind her long fringe.

"Can we give them their medallions?" Megan called to Lauren.

"No, wait for me and Buster. Here, Buster. *Please* come and sit!"

"OK, well I'm putting my badge on anyway," Megan decided. She pinned it to her T-shirt.

"Me too." Caitlin grinned as Buster ran between Lauren's legs. "Put your badge on, Lauren!" she called.

While Lauren chased Buster, Megan handed Caitlin a camera. "Can you take a picture of me and Dylan?"

"Sure," said Caitlin. "Look at me. Smile!" *Click*. She got a perfect snap of the proud owner and her puppy.

"And me!" Lauren said. She'd finally caught Buster and now held him tight to her chest as Caitlin took the photo. He wriggled, then licked her face. *Click*.

"Let me take one of you and Daisy," Lauren offered. *Click*. Now all three members of the Puppy Club had pictures of themselves with their pups.

"*Now* can we give them their medallions?" Megan asked.

Lauren set Buster down beside Daisy and Dylan. "Si-i-it!" she told him. For once he did as he was told.

The three puppies sat in a row, looking totally sweet. Megan, Lauren and Caitlin knelt in front of them.

"Ready?" Megan asked. She handed Lauren and Caitlin a piece of paper with the Puppy Club promises clearly listed.

"We are members of the Magic Mountain Puppy Club," the girls read together in serious voices. "We promise to look after our puppies well. We promise to take them to puppy training classes. We promise to feed them and play with them. We promise to take them for long walks."

Dylan cocked his head to one side. Buster wagged his tail. Daisy's bright eyes shone. They seemed to like the sound of that.

"OK?" Caitlin whispered.

"OK!" Lauren and Megan agreed.

Together they leant forward and hung the gold medallions around their puppies' necks.

Daisy glanced up at Caitlin and twitched her little black nose.

"D-d-did you see that?" Caitlin gasped. Maybe she'd imagined it.

Buster pricked his ears and sniffed the air. His gold medallion swung from his neck.

"I feel like I'm floating!" Megan whispered.

"Weird!" Lauren said. As she'd leant forward to hang Buster's medallion around his neck, she'd started to feel dizzy. Now the lawn seemed to tilt more steeply and the trees above their heads grew blurry.

"D-D-Daisy moved!" Caitlin stammered. She shook her head as if to clear it.

The little toy dog opened her mouth and barked. The girls looked at her in amazement.

"I feel dizzy!" Lauren said, struggling to her feet.

The trees and lawn spun around. "What's happening?"

"I'm floating!" Megan cried. She and Dylan rose from the ground. She looked down at the neat flower beds. "We're spinning around!"

"Wow!" Caitlin cried. "Daisy's come to life!"

"Buster, come back!" Lauren yelled. She saw him race off and get caught up in a brilliant white light.

Then the light surrounded them, too, and everything went blurry as the girls spun around and around . . .

CHAPTER THREE

"Sleuth City News!" a voice cried from a long way off, growing louder as Megan, Lauren and Caitlin finally stopped spinning. "Read all about it! Pampered Pooch Hijacked from Handbag!"

"Sleuth City?" Megan said in wonder.

"W-w-where are we? What's all this about?"

"Owner offers big reward!" the newspaper seller cried.

Caitlin looked up at the tallest, shiniest buildings she'd ever seen. Then she stared along a street crowded with traffic. "Sleuth City?" she murmured.

"Wow, magic!" Lauren cried, chasing after Buster as he hurtled towards a crowd of people gathered on the pavement.

Sensible Megan kept Dylan safely by her side. Cities were dangerous places for dogs – they could easily get lost or run over. She went up to the newspaper stand and studied the big headline.

"Pampered Pooch Hijacked from Handbag!" she read out loud to Caitlin.

"Ten-year-old heiress, May Blossom Jerome's much-loved pet, Peaches, was dognapped earlier today. Thieves snatched the pedigree pooch from May Blossom's Gucci handbag, leaving her hysterical. Her multi-millionaire dad, Rob Jerome, has offered a $100,000 reward for Peaches' safe return."

Caitlin took a deep breath and kept a tight hold of her own puppy. "Did you hear that, Daisy?" she whispered. "A pup has been dognapped!"

The little Yorkie pricked her ears. She squirmed in Caitlin's arms.

"Are you kids going to buy that newspaper, or not?" the man at the stall demanded.

"Er – no thanks." Megan stepped back.

"I can't work this out," she told Caitlin. "How did we get here? Is it something to do with our Puppy Club?"

Caitlin narrowed her eyes. "The man at Magic Mountain said these were special puppies. Which means *anything* could happen. And Daisy has already come to life, just like I wished!"

"So is that what you think it is – magic?" Megan asked in amazement.

Caitlin nodded. "For me, it's a dream come true!"

Just then, Lauren yelled from down the street. She had hold of Buster's collar as he yapped at the crowd. "Come over here!

There are TV cameras and reporters and everything!" So Caitlin and Megan went with Dylan and Daisy towards the wide glass entrance of a high-rise office block. A man in a dark suit stood in front the building, his arm around a young girl with long blonde hair. Cameras pointed and bright lights shone on them. The man had a tanned face and a trim grey beard.

"May Blossom and I have come back here, to the scene of the crime, to appeal for witnesses," he explained. "Someone must have seen or heard something. We want anyone with information to come forward and help the police to recover my daughter's pet dog."

"Mr Jerome, is it true that you're offering a $100,000 reward?" a TV reporter asked.

"May Blossom, how do you feel about losing your puppy?" someone else called.

May Blossom Jerome stood with tears in her blue eyes. Her bottom lip trembled.

"How do you *suppose* she feels?" Lauren muttered, as Buster sniffed around in the gutter where black bin bags were stacked, ready for collection. She turned to Caitlin and Megan. "Hey, wouldn't it be great if we could help May Blossom – you know, pick up some clues and solve the crime? After all, our puppies *are* magic and we're in Sleuth City! 'Sleuth' as in 'detective', meaning mysteries and crimes to solve!"

"You're crazy!" Megan said.

"Imagine how *you'd* feel if it was Dylan who'd been snatched," Lauren said.

Megan bent down to hug her black Labrador pup. "I know I'd feel horrible!" she admitted.

"Yes, but…" Caitlin said nervously.

Under the TV lights, Rob Jerome and his daughter were ending their interview and heading for a nearby limo. The TV crews packed up their gear.

"How on earth can we solve this dognap?" Megan demanded.

"Yeah, how?" Caitlin echoed. She felt sorry for May Blossom and wanted to help. She just didn't see what they could do.

Just then, Buster shoved his nose between two bin bags and grabbed a small object between his jaws. He carried it straight over to Lauren.

"What's that?" she asked, stooping to take it from him.

Meanwhile, Rob Jerome and his daughter were pushing their way through the crowd. They bumped into Caitlin and startled Daisy.

"Yap!" Daisy yelped. May Blossom Jerome stopped dead. She stared at the little Yorkie, shook her head, then stared again.

"Yap-yap!" Daisy gave a high-pitched bark.

"Peaches!" May Blossom gasped. "Is that you?"

Caitlin stepped back in horror. "No, this is Daisy. We're not from around here—" she began.

But May Blossom had already lunged forward and snatched the puppy. "Peaches!" she cried. "It is - it's my darling poochie. Daddy, it's Peaches! She's come back!"

CHAPTER FOUR

"No – wait! Don't take her!" Caitlin wailed.

She watched, helpless, as May Blossom disappeared into her dad's limo with the struggling Daisy. Breathlessly, Caitlin followed them.

"She's not your puppy," she gasped. "Look, she's wearing a Magic Mountain medallion. She belongs to our Puppy Club!"

Rob Jerome leant out of the window of their gleaming black car. "If my daughter thinks that this is her puppy, then that's who it is," he snapped, ordering the driver to move away.

But Megan and Dylan bravely blocked the car's way. The chauffeur scowled at them.

"What do you kids want? Oh yeah, the $100,000," Mr Jerome said, reaching for his cheque book.

May Blossom held Daisy tight. "Peaches is a Yorkie, just like this," she insisted. "She's exactly this size, with a cute tuft of silver hair that falls over her eyes, and she has one brown ear and one silvery-blue . . . oh!"

Daisy pricked up her two brown ears. "Yap!"

"See!" Caitlin cried, seizing Daisy back again. Her happy puppy licked her cheek.

May Blossom burst into tears. "It's not Peaches after all!" she cried. "Oh, it's so unfair!"

Her dad frowned and put his cheque book back in his pocket. "Let's get out of here," he told the driver.

Megan and Dylan stepped back on to the pavement. They watched May Blossom's tears flow again as the car drove away.

"Look what Buster found amongst the bin bags!" Lauren came running up to Megan and Caitlin. She showed them a shiny new mobile phone, turning it over in her hands. "Maybe it's a clue!"

Megan groaned. She had a feeling that May Blossom was spoiled rotten, but then that wasn't poor Peaches' fault. "Uh-oh, Lauren's already hot on the dognapper's trail!" she said.

"Maybe she is," Caitlin decided. "I mean, how come a nice new phone got thrown into the gutter?"

As the girls talked, Dylan, Buster and Daisy sat quietly on the pavement. They looked up at their owners and waited.

"How do we know it got *thrown* there?" Megan argued. "It could have just fallen out of someone's bag."

Wag-wag went the puppies' tails as they waited patiently.

Then Lauren snapped her fingers. "I've got it! It fell out of May Blossom's bag when Peaches was dognapped!" Buster barked in approval. Lauren handed the phone to Megan. "Do you know how to switch it on?"

Behind her, a car swerved clear of the traffic and dropped off its passenger by a subway entrance. A yellow taxi hooted its horn.

"Buster thinks it belongs to May Blossom," Lauren insisted. "Don't you, Buster?"

He wagged his tail harder still.

"OK, let me see," Megan said, pressing a button. The menu appeared. She selected **SHORT MESSAGE** and **INBOX**.

PLEASE WAIT, the phone asked.

"Hurry up!" Lauren insisted. "I want to read the last message in the inbox."

"Why?" Caitlin wanted to know.

"It might give us more clues." An excited Lauren snatched the phone back. "'**HEY MB**'," she read. "'**MAKE SURE U WALK 2 SKOOL 2DAY. DON'T USE THE LIMO. TRUST ME - LAYLA XXX**' – Huh?"

"MB?" Caitlin frowned. Then her eyes lit up. "Hey, you were right, Lauren. MB is May Blossom! This *is* her phone!"

Buster, Dylan and Daisy pricked up their ears, ready for action.

"See!" Lauren cried. "It's a mega-clue! Good dog, Buster!"

Even Megan began to believe it. "Why shouldn't May Blossom drive to school this morning?" she asked. "And who's Layla?"

"We don't know – yet!" Lauren muttered. She was thinking hard.

"Anyway, it looks like May Blossom ignored Layla's message," Megan pointed out. "She went to school by car and that's when her puppy got snatched from her handbag."

"Which means Layla was trying to warn May Blossom," Caitlin cut in. "So now we need to find this Layla and talk to her."

"But how?" Megan and Lauren said together.

The three girls frowned and looked down at their bright-eyed pups.

Dylan jumped to his feet and snatched the

phone from Megan. Then he quickly set off at a trot.

"Dylan, where are you going?" Lauren called. She watched as Daisy and Buster trotted after him.

"I think he's picked up a scent," Megan said. "That's what Labradors are good at!"

Caitlin nodded. "And Daisy and Buster definitely want to go with him."

Lauren watched the three pups trotting briskly along the pavement. "Let's follow them!" she gasped. "Quick, before we lose them!"

CHAPTER FIVE

Dylan led the way. The black Labrador pup headed along the city streets, nose to the ground, picking up the trail.

Scruffy Buster romped along behind, weaving between shoppers and office workers, almost tripping them up as he darted after Dylan.

At the corner of the street, dainty Daisy turned to check that Caitlin, Lauren and Megan were following.

"It's OK, we're coming," Caitlin called, as the red signal turned to green and the puppies crossed the road.

"It looks like the pups know where they're going," Megan said.

"For sure." Lauren and Caitlin nodded, then sprinted to catch up with them.

Sniff-sniff. Dylan followed the scent. *Snuffle-snuffle.* Buster scooted between a forest of legs and feet.

"Yap!" Daisy turned to wait for Caitlin.

At last Dylan came to a stop and the girls finally caught up with their puppies. They all gazed up at the glass apartment building in front of them.

"Jerome Towers." Caitlin read out the name above the entrance. "This must be where May Blossom lives with her mega-rich dad."

"Wow, Dylan, you're a super-pup!" Megan exclaimed, taking the phone back from him.

"Come back, Buster!" Lauren cried as her scatty puppy made a dash inside the building. "Not so much super-pup as snooper-pup!" She wished that for once her little mongrel would sit and wait until they had decided what to do next.

But it was no good – Buster was already racing across the shiny floor. A man at the reception desk yelled for him to stop. There was the *ding!* of a bell and some lift doors opened.

"Uh-oh!" Lauren groaned as Buster jumped into the lift. She ran after him. The lift doors closed.

"They've gone!" Caitlin gasped, watching the green arrow next to the lift point downwards.

The desk man rushed towards them. "Get out of here, you kids!" he yelled. "And take your dogs with you!"

Caitlin, Daisy, Megan and Dylan high-tailed it back into the street.

"The lift went down to the basement," Megan said. She crouched beside Dylan and looked him in the eye. "Find!" she said.

Dylan wagged his tail. And off he went, along the pavement, around the side of Jerome Towers, until he found a sloping entrance down into an underground car park.

"Good boy!" Megan was hard on his heels. The black Labrador puppy disappeared between rows of parked cars, tail wagging.

Suddenly, they heard tyres squealing and the sound of hard braking.

Caitlin gasped and picked Daisy up.

"Dylan!" Megan called in alarm, running

after him. She saw a red car swerve and miss the puppy by inches. Calmly the little Labrador ran on towards the lift.

Just as . . . *ding!* The lift doors opened and Lauren and Buster stepped out.

"What kept you?" Lauren grinned at her Puppy Club friends. "We've been going up and down in this lift for ages!"

"OK, let's think!" Megan insisted. They had gathered by the lift doors to make their next plan.

Caitlin tried to clear her head and get things in order. "So, this is where May Blossom and her dad live . . ." she began.

"Probably," Megan added cautiously.

"Which means their black stretch limo must be down here somewhere," Caitlin said, ignoring her friend's doubts.

"Maybe. Maybe not." Megan never liked to jump to conclusions. "What if Mr Jerome is out at work right now?"

It was Lauren's turn to chip in. "But Dylan led us here," she pointed out. "He must have had a good reason."

Megan nodded. Already she trusted her pup. "So, what are we looking for now we're here?"

"The black limo!" Caitlin and Lauren agreed.

Dylan, Daisy and Buster pricked up their ears.

Together they set off along the rows of parked cars until they came to a space marked **'PRIVATE. RESERVED FOR MR JEROME.'** Then they yelped and barked for the girls to join them.

"No limo!" Lauren sighed as she reached the empty bay.

"But listen!" Caitlin held a finger to her lips. She'd heard the swish of tyres on the smooth

tarmac and the low throb of a car engine.

Before the girls and their pups had time to move, a big black car cruised into view.

The driver saw them and braked suddenly. Then he opened the door and stepped out. He marched towards them in his grey driver's uniform, frowning fiercely. "Not you kids again!" he muttered, hands on hips. "Why can't you just leave well alone?"

CHAPTER SIX

"Did you see the way Buster growled at him?" Lauren whispered, proud of her fierce little pup.

The girls and their puppies were back in the lift, safe from Eddie, the angry driver, who'd stormed off after giving them a real earful about playing at detectives. Megan pressed the button for the Ground Floor.

"Yeah, the pups hated him," Caitlin agreed. She'd kept tight hold of Daisy all the time that Eddie had been yelling – not for her pup's safety, but for Eddie's. The little Yorkie had growled as long as the man kept on yelling.

"He just wouldn't listen! Even though we explained that we were trying to help May Blossom to find Peaches," Lauren said angrily.

"Don't waste my time!" he'd shouted. "I've just dropped my boss at an important business meeting. And now I've got stuff to do! I don't need you and your stupid puppies following me around!"

"He wouldn't even tell us where May Blossom is so we can talk to her!" Lauren stuck out her bottom lip in a big sulk. "Sometimes people can be really unhelpful!"

The lift jolted to a halt and the doors slid open. The girls and their pups stepped out into the huge lobby.

A small, dark-haired girl stood by the glass door, holding her mobile phone. She pressed some buttons, and the shiny May Blossom phone in Lauren's pocket started to ring! Lauren took it out and answered it.

"Hey, May Blossom," the girl by the door said. "How are you doing? It's Layla calling you from down in the lobby – you know, Eddie's daughter!"

Grinning from ear to ear, Lauren rushed impulsively up to Layla, May Blossom's phone in hand. "Hi. How lucky is this? I'm Lauren, and this is Megan and Caitlin. We need to talk to you!"

The puppies sniffed at Layla's shoes and wagged their tails.

Layla frowned at the pups, then at the girls. "How come you've got May Blossom's phone?" she asked suspiciously.

"It's a long story," Caitlin said.

"Did you steal it?"

"No way." Megan frowned back. "Whose side do you think we're on?"

Lauren jumped in again. "We're trying to help," she explained. "My dog, Buster, found the phone by some bin bags, near to where May Blossom's dog, Peaches, was dognapped."

Layla stared at them. She tucked a strand of her short black hair behind an ear and tugged at the bright orange T-shirt hanging over her jeans.

"Back off, Lauren," Megan said quietly. She'd picked up the worried look in Layla's dark brown eyes. "The thing is, Layla – we just want to know why you sent a message warning

May Blossom not to drive to school this morning."

"Woof!" Dylan agreed. He wanted to know the answer to that too.

"Did you know something bad was going to happen?" Caitlin asked.

Layla blushed, then shook her head. "No way. Now, just give me the phone, will you?"

As Layla made a grab for May Blossom's phone, Buster jumped up and snatched it, then ran off with it into a safe corner.

"Come on, Layla," Lauren insisted. "We just heard you say that Eddie's your dad. He drives the limo. He knew about the dognap before it happened, didn't he?"

Layla didn't answer. Instead, she panicked and fled towards the lift.

This time it was Daisy and Dylan who cut her off, yapping at her ankles.

"Call them off!" Layla pleaded, her back pinned against the wall.

"Only if you answer our questions," said Lauren.

"OK," Layla admitted slowly. "My dad *did* see some shady guys hanging around the car park yesterday."

"So?" Megan prompted. She could see that Layla's situation was tricky. No way would she want to get her dad into trouble, yet it was obvious she knew more than she was saying.

"So he got rid of them. But not before he overheard them talking about Peaches and May Blossom."

"What exactly did they say?" Caitlin asked.

Layla's frown deepened. "Stuff about having orders to snatch the dog."

"Wow!" Lauren gasped. "That's mega-important. Why didn't your dad tell Mr Jerome?"

Layla sighed. "I guess he thought they were joking. He told my mum and me when he got home from work last night. Mum said to forget it. But I thought it might be serious, so I decided to send a message to May Blossom."

"And it turned out they were wrong and you were right," Megan said quietly.

"Yes, but what do I do now?" Layla asked, close to tears. "I mean, I really want the cops to find poor little Peaches, but I can't land my dad in a whole heap of trouble, can I?"

CHAPTER SEVEN

Caitlin thought for a while. "Your dad made a mistake, that's all. And the sooner the police know about those men hanging about in the car park, the better. Mr Jerome will understand."

But Layla shook her head and began to cry. "You don't know him," she sobbed. "Rob Jerome is really tough. My dad will lose his job over this for sure!"

"So you came to see May Blossom instead?" As usual, Megan had thought ahead.

Layla nodded. "I like her. She doesn't have many friends, so at a time like this she needs me."

"So what now?" Lauren looked at Caitlin and Megan.

Before they could reply, bouncy Buster backed away from the lift doors, crouched, then ran at the control panel. He jumped up and neatly tapped the button with his paw. The doors slid open.

"Whoa!" Layla gasped, as if she couldn't believe her eyes.

"I guess that answers the question!" Lauren laughed. She herded everyone into the lift and pressed the button. "It looks like Buster wants us to go up and have a talk with May Blossom – so that's exactly what we're going to do!"

"Which floor?" Caitlin asked, her finger poised over the control panel.

"May Blossom lives in the penthouse," Layla replied in a wobbly voice.

Caitlin pressed the top button and the lift went up. When they stepped out, they were in a lobby surrounded on all sides by glass. The whole of Sleuth City was spread out beneath them.

But there was no time to admire the view, as Dylan, Buster and Daisy crowded round the door leading to the Jeromes' apartment. Dylan put a paw up and scratched at the door, while Daisy gave a sharp bark which brought May Blossom running.

"Peaches!" Rob Jerome's daughter flung open the door with high hopes. She looked down at Daisy, then up at Caitlin. "Oh, it's you again," she said glumly, her face full of disappointment.

"Sorry, yes – it's only us." Caitlin picked Daisy up.

Then May Blossom spotted Layla.

"Why have you brought these people here?" she demanded. "Who are they?"

"Time to talk!" Lauren said to Layla, marching her through the penthouse door.

Caitlin perched with Daisy on a white leather sofa. Megan stood by a wide window overlooking a gleaming river. Lauren and Layla faced May Blossom across a glass coffee table. In the background, a plasma TV screen showed a boring quiz show.

"So now you know," Layla told May Blossom, sniffing back her tears. "My dad caught some guys snooping around and we never told you!"

"And I never read your message," May Blossom admitted. She wore a pink top with a frill around the neck. Her designer jeans were cut off below the knee.

"Well, there's no point thinking about that now," Megan cut in. May Blossom was definitely a bit of a Pampered Princess, with her diamond stud earrings and silver chain necklace – but however spoilt she was, she loved her puppy, just like they loved theirs. And in Megan's book, that made her OK. "That's all in the past. We have to plan ahead."

For once, Buster and Dylan didn't seem interested in the girls' talk. After they'd padded around the apartment, sniffing at this and that, the two pups sat down in front of the TV. Buster flopped his head on to his paws and yawned, while Dylan sat quietly, tail gently thumping the floor.

"Your pooch is so-o-o cute!" May Blossom said to Caitlin, stroking Daisy's soft fur. She sighed. "Just like my adorable Peaches!"

"Oh, May Blossom, I feel so bad," Layla said. "I know how much you love that pup!"

"Please don't cry!" Lauren begged, as she saw May Blossom's bottom lip tremble. "Like Megan said, we just have to work out who those two men were and why they'd want to dognap Peaches."

In front of the TV, Buster and Dylan whined at the theme tune that brought the quiz to an end. Then they yapped excitedly at the loud music that introduced the News.

"I'll turn it off," May Blossom suggested, sniffing. She reached for the remote.

"Breaking news from Sleuth City!" the female newsreader began.

The two puppies stood up and wagged their tails, giving sharp barks at the screen.

"No, don't switch it off!" Megan said. She realised the puppies were trying to tell them something. She took the remote control away from May Blossom.

"One of the biggest money deals in history is on the brink of collapse," the newsreader continued. "Millionaire Rob Jerome has failed to show up for an early morning meeting in Sleuth City with the owners of Galaxy 3, the computer game that has reached number one in the world market."

"Your dad's on the news!" Caitlin gasped at May Blossom, pointing to the screen, which was showing a picture of Mr Jerome relaxing on his yacht.

"Hush!" Megan warned.

"Rob Jerome's business rival, Henry King, is said to be in Sleuth City, ready to snatch the deal for himself." Now the TV screen showed a young, blonde man getting out of a private helicopter surrounded by bodyguards. "If King beats Jerome to Galaxy 3, he'll be worth a billion dollars," the newsreader said.

"Oh, I get it!" Megan said, putting the TV on mute as the News moved on.

"You do?" Lauren said, confused.

May Blossom, Layla, Lauren and Caitlin waited for Megan to explain.

"It's obvious," she told them. "May Blossom, your dad had to be at a meeting early this morning, yes?"

May Blossom shrugged. "I guess so."

"But he didn't make it because of all this stuff with your puppy."

"So?"

"So, he keeps the Galaxy 3 people waiting and they get annoyed." Megan couldn't understand why the others still didn't get it. "And doesn't it seem weird that Henry King just happens to be on the spot, right then and there, ready to sign the deal in your dad's place and earn himself a billion dollars?"

"Yeah, big coincidence!" Caitlin and Lauren agreed, suddenly seeing what Megan was getting at.

"Which means that King didn't want your

dad to make it to the meeting in the first place," Megan explained carefully to May Blossom.

"What are you saying?" May Blossom demanded, as the light slowly dawned.

Megan spread her hands palms upwards. "I'm saying Henry King snatched Peaches because he knew it would make your dad late for the meeting."

"Henry King!" May Blossom and Layla whispered.

Megan nodded. "Yup, I'm convinced he's your dognapper. Now all we have to do is prove it. Let's find out where he's staying!"

CHAPTER EIGHT

Buster, Dylan and Daisy crowded round the penthouse door, ready for action.

"Which is the most expensive hotel in town?" Megan asked May Blossom. "Where do all the rich people go?"

"That would be the Park Central," May Blossom said. "It's where the celebs stay. There's even a heli-pad for guests with their own 'copters."

"I bet that's where Henry King is booked in," said Caitlin, as she joined the pups at the door. "Come on, let's go!"

"Wait!" May Blossom ran into her bedroom to fetch a jacket. "I'm coming too!"

"No way!" Lauren cried. She didn't want May Blossom and Layla slowing them down. "You two have to stay here, in case the dognappers try to phone the apartment."

"Why would they do that?" May Blossom wanted to know.

"To demand loads of money before they let you have Peaches back," Caitlin explained.

"Look after May Blossom," Megan told Layla. "We'll call you as soon as we can."

The three Puppy Club pals shot out of the penthouse behind Buster, Daisy and Dylan. They ran for the lift and headed for the ground floor, across the reception lobby and out on to the crowded street.

"Which way to the Park Central Hotel?" Megan gasped at a taxi driver parked by the kerb.

"Straight up City Avenue, take a left on to Park Road," he spluttered through a mouthful of burger.

Buster was already romping ahead, darting in and out between legs and lamp posts, following the trail that would solve the mystery of the missing pooch.

"Wait for us!" Lauren called in vain after the livewire brown pup.

Megan kept up with Dylan, who had his nose to the ground as usual. Caitlin scooped up Daisy and followed.

"Sleuth City latest!" a newspaper seller called. "Stand-off between Jerome and King for Galaxy 3! Jerome shows up late. Who will sign the deal?"

"Woof!" Buster stopped at the corner of Park Road to wait for the others.

Meanwhile, Lauren dug into her pocket to answer her mobile.

"Yep," she said. "OK, I got that. Wait a second, May Blossom, while I tell the others."

"What is it?" Megan asked, joining Buster and Lauren at the corner of Park Road. Not too far ahead, there was a huge green space with railings, trees and pathways.

"May Blossom's on the phone. The dognappers just called her."

"What did they say?" Caitlin arrived out of breath, with Daisy safe under her arm.

Lauren frowned. "They said to tell her dad that if he went ahead and signed the deal, she'd never see Peaches again."

"That's cruel!" Caitlin gasped. "So what does May Blossom do now?"

"I don't know," Lauren replied. 'She's in a real mess – crying down the phone and everything."

Megan thought a while, then spoke clearly. "Get her to call the dognappers back and say her dad's phone is switched off and she's left

66

an urgent message for him to call her back."

"Cool," Lauren nodded. "That'll buy us a bit more time." She passed on the message to a tearful May Blossom.

"And look, there's the hotel!" Eagerly Caitlin pointed to the row of tall, bright flags fluttering outside a massive building made of glass and steel. Already Buster and Dylan were trotting ahead, only stopping when they reached the green-and-gold canopy stretching over the pavement.

A hotel doorman in a green-and-gold uniform spotted the pups. "Scoot!" he said.

Buster sat under the canopy and pricked his ears. Dylan sniffed at the bottom step leading up to the hotel.

"I said, scoot!" the doorman repeated, aiming a small kick at Buster.

Buster growled.

"Little mutt – so you think you're tough?" the doorman muttered. He looked up to see Lauren. "Does this dog belong to you?"

Before Lauren could answer, the hotel doors swished open and a woman in a bright yellow dress and big sunglasses came out. The doorman quickly shooed Lauren and Buster out of the way.

"Hey, that's Candy Price, the supermodel!" someone yelled from across the street.

"Oh, wow! Yeah, that's her! Hey, Candy, can I have your autograph?"

Candy swept down the steps, followed by four bodyguards wearing dark glasses. A big crowd was gathering. Candy posed for pictures, scribbled her name a couple of times, then glided on into a waiting limo.

"You still here?" the doorman grunted at Lauren and Buster. He glanced down the street to see Megan hurrying to join them, and Dylan. "I already told you, get out of here. You'll give the place a bad name with that mutt!"

"Wow, here comes Jay Sayers!" A star-spotter in the crowd had recognised the famous movie actor following Candy down the steps.

The crowd moved in for more photos. It gave Dylan and Buster a chance to sneak past the doorman. But there was another man in a uniform guarding the entrance.

"Hey, girls, come and get your pups before I send for the van to take them off to the stray dogs' home," the second doorman yelled as Sayers joined Candy in the limo. "They wouldn't like that one little bit, believe me!"

Lauren and Megan sprinted up the steps and grabbed Buster and Dylan. They picked them up and kept a firm hold.

"What are you talking about?" Lauren demanded. "They're not strays. Anyone can see that they belong to us!"

Megan pulled Lauren and Buster back down the steps.

"Scruffy little mutt!" The first doorman scowled at Buster.

But then Caitlin swung into action. She swept up the steps with Daisy. "Who are you calling nasty names?" she demanded in a spoiled, May Blossom-type voice.

Lauren and Megan turned to stare at Caitlin.

Caitlin looked down her nose at the two doormen. "Don't you know who I am?"

"No. But I guess you're going to tell me," the first doorman sneered.

Caitlin tossed her long red hair. "I'm May Blossom Jerome and these are my friends!"

Wow! Lauren's mouth fell open. Megan gasped, then secretly crossed her fingers. This was some risk that Caitlin was taking!

The first doorman narrowed his eyes and looked closely at Caitlin and Daisy. He seemed unsure. "Run that by me again."

Caitlin tutted. "May Blossom Jerome. My father is Rob Jerome. Everybody in Sleuth City knows us."

Slowly, the doorman decided she was genuine. He grovelled big time. "Of course, Miss Jerome. I'm sorry, Miss Jerome."

Caitlin stroked Daisy. "There, there, Peaches. Did the nasty man upset my poor little pooch?"

"Peaches!" the doorman echoed. "Isn't that – didn't she – wasn't she—?"

"Dognapped?" Caitlin cut in. "Exactly. Poor Peaches has had a horrid day. That's why the first thing I decided to do when I got her back was to bring her downtown to a dog beauty parlour. You do have one here at the hotel, don't you?"

"We do," the doorman hastily replied, falling over himself to lead Caitlin up the steps and open the door. "The Pampered Pets parlour is in the basement, next door to the Fitness Centre."

"Wow!" Lauren said out loud this time.

"Yeah, wow!" Megan murmured. Her shy friend Caitlin had played Little Miss Snooty to perfection.

No one said another word as first Caitlin and Daisy, then Lauren and Buster, Megan and Dylan swept through the wide open doors of the Park Central Hotel.

CHAPTER NINE

"Would you look at that!" In the basement of the hotel, Lauren peered through a door leading to an Olympic-size pool with fountains and chutes.

"And this!" Megan stopped outside a gym full of shiny machines and weights.

Caitlin went ahead with Daisy, Buster and Dylan. She found the Pampered Pets parlour and marched straight in.

"Wait for us!" Lauren and Megan called.

Inside the parlour there was a row of soft doggy cushions and a woman in a lilac uniform. She came up to Caitlin and Daisy, dog-brush in hand.

Buster and Dylan spied the luxury cushions and quickly curled up for a nap. Time to take a break from the hard work of tracking down Peaches!

Meanwhile Caitlin handed Daisy over to the assistant. "I'd like you to brush her and tie a cute little bow to keep the hair out of her eyes," she said in her May Blossom voice.

The woman got to work on Daisy.

Lauren drew Caitlin to one side. "Wow, you're good!" she whispered. "You should join the school drama club when we get back!"

Caitlin blushed. "It worked pretty well," she admitted. "Now that we're inside the hotel, all we have to do is work out where Henry King is staying. We can set Buster and Dylan to work again!"

"You think?" Megan pointed to the snoozing pups.

"Yap!" Daisy protested as the woman tugged at her hair.

Buster and Dylan each opened one eye.

Just then the door opened and a broad-shouldered man in a black T-shirt and jeans came in. He looked awkward and out of place in this perfumed doggy world of pampering and treats. "Hey," he muttered to the girls. Then he went across to the assistant. "Uh-hum. . ."

She looked up from tying a pink ribbon in Daisy's hair. "Yes?"

"My boss is staying in the Garden Suite and we forgot to bring food for his dog," he said. "She's getting kind of hungry."

Lauren, Megan and Caitlin listened eagerly. The Garden Suite . . . a hungry dog . . . Could this be the break they were looking for?

"We don't keep food here," the assistant

said snootily. "Try the grocery store down the street."

The man grunted his thanks and went off.

"The Garden Suite. Let's go!" Lauren whispered. She called Buster, who was wide awake now and came running.

"Wait!" Megan wanted to be sure before they dashed off. Could it be true? The man didn't name his boss, but he could easily have meant Henry King. And the Garden Suite made sense too – it was right by the hotel's heli-pad, making it easy for King to fly in and out.

"Yep," she finally agreed, calling Dylan to her side. "It's worth a try. Let's go!"

'**GARDEN**'. There was a sign on the wall with an arrow pointing towards a door.

Lauren, Caitlin and Megan ran with their pups along the wide corridor. They burst out of the hotel into the garden. Buster sniffed the air. Dylan's nose went straight to the ground.

He followed a dozen different scents.

"Look!" Caitlin hung onto Daisy and pointed towards a black helicopter parked on the pad. "There's a gold crown painted on the side."

"Crown equals king!" Megan worked it out. "*Henry* King. It must be his logo!"

Sniff-sniff! Buster and Dylan trotted through the flower beds. They nosed their way towards a wide patio lined with spiky plants in giant pots.

A man appeared at a nearby window and banged on it to scare off the pups.

With a gasp, Lauren, Megan and Caitlin ducked down out of sight.

"That's not the man from the dog parlour," Lauren hissed from behind a raised flower bed. Though he wore a similar black T-shirt and jeans, this man was taller and thinner.

"No, the other one went to buy food," Megan reminded her. "Let's hope this guy didn't see us."

Sniff! Dylan ignored the man at the window.

He was picking up scents and wagging his tail, while Buster romped around the patio, barking wildly.

"Buster, what are you doing?" Lauren hissed. "You'll give us away!"

But the excited pup barked and yelped like crazy.

Caitlin risked raising her head above the flower bed. Through a cloud of yellow roses she saw the man slide open the French doors.

"Get out of here, you noisy nutcase!" he yelled at Buster. "Jeez, I hate dogs!"

As he shouted and waved his arms at Buster, Dylan sneaked in through the doors.

"Buster's grabbed the man's attention and Dylan's gone inside!" Caitlin reported.

"Oh no, what if they catch him?" Behind the flower bed, Megan held her breath. "One–two–three–four…" She counted the seconds until Dylan reappeared.

"Now the man's picked up a garden chair and he's holding it over Buster," Caitlin said. "He's trying to hit him with it, but he's missed."

"Phew!" Lauren breathed a sigh of relief.

". . .five–six–seven–eight," Megan counted. Come back, Dylan!

Buster ran circles around the clumsy man. Meanwhile Dylan's face peered out through the glass door.

"Dylan's OK!" Caitlin hissed.

"Thank goodness!" Megan breathed again.

"He's coming out. He's bringing someone with him!"

The clever Labrador pup trotted on to the patio followed by a tiny, long-haired dog. Her silky grey and light-brown hair was

so long it touched the ground. She wore a top-knot tied with a yellow ribbon.

"It's… it's a little Yorkie!" Caitlin gasped.

Lauren and Megan couldn't help it – they rose to their feet and jumped for joy.

"Peaches!" they cried.

CHAPTER TEN

Peaches Jerome made a bee-line for Caitlin and Daisy.

The dognapper spotted the three girls. He ran towards them. Soon he was joined by the man they'd seen in the Pampered Pets salon.

"Lee, if we lose this pooch, we're in trouble!" he yelled, throwing down his grocery bag and racing towards the yellow roses. "Mr King will fire us on the spot!"

"So, why are you standing there?" the tall dognapper demanded. "Come on, Matt, I need some help here!"

Right then, Caitlin had another brilliant

idea. With Daisy's hair tied up in a ribbon, she was sure her own pup could easily be mistaken for Peaches. So she scooped Peaches up and set Daisy down instead. Daisy raced to help Buster and Dylan.

Buster darted between Lee's legs and tripped him up. The dognapper went sprawling across the patio. Dylan and Daisy rushed at Matt and seized his trouser legs. They tugged with all their might.

Both men went down. But they quickly scrambled to their feet and made a grab for the pups. They pounced and missed. Buster, Daisy and Dylan were too quick, and the dognappers too clumsy.

"Go, Dylan! Yes, good boy!" Megan cheered her clever Labrador pup as he swerved and wriggled between two flower tubs, just out of reach.

"Trip them up, Buster!" Lauren yelled.

"It's OK, Peaches, we've saved you!" Caitlin murmured to the trembling dog she now held in her arms. She watched her own little Daisy run right between Matt's legs.

"Hey, there she is!" Lee spun round and chased Daisy. "Peaches, come back here!"

Caitlin smiled grimly at his mistake. Daisy made a great decoy, heading back into the hotel and down a flight of steps towards the Fitness Centre.

Buster and Dylan bounded after her, quickly followed by the dognappers.

"Come back, you stupid mutt!" they yelled.

Megan, Lauren and Caitlin paused to discuss tactics.

"You wait here with Peaches," Megan suggested to Caitlin. "It's safer."

"No way!" That was Daisy in there, being chased by two thugs! Caitlin didn't plan to let her out of her sight.

So the three girls set off after the men with Peaches hidden under Caitlin's T-shirt.

"Grab that Yorkie!" Lee yelled at the assistant who came to the door of the Pampered Pets salon to see what all the noise was about.

But the snooty woman took one look at the

chaos in the corridor, then stepped right back inside and closed the door.

"Stop that dog!" Matt cried at a chambermaid pushing a linen trolley.

Daisy raced under the trolley and sprinted on. Buster and Dylan swerved around it.

Crash! Lee and Matt blundered straight into the trolley, sending neatly stacked towels and sheets flying.

As the two dognappers lay flat out on the carpet, Caitlin, Lauren and Megan jumped over them. They caught up with the pups at the entrance to the swimming pool.

Now Matt and Lee were up again, grunting and panting, and angrier than ever.

Dylan and Buster looked at each other, then bounded forward and jumped up at the swimming pool door. It swung open and they vanished inside.

Meanwhile it seemed to the men that Peaches sat in the entrance, ears pricked, waiting.

"Sit! Stay! Don't move!" They sprinted towards her. This was their chance – May Blossom's pooch was gazing up at them, her dark brown eyes sparkling, her pink ribbon neatly keeping her top-knot in place.

"Grab her!" Lee cried.

"I'm trying!" Matt yelled, as Daisy jumped up, nimbly turned and raced towards the edge of the pool, where she came to a screeching halt.

Matt and Lee charged after her. Hidden behind the door, Buster and Dylan leapt out, yapping and barking, snapping at the dognappers' ankles.

The men threw up their arms and tried to keep their balance. But Buster and Dylan were between their legs. The dognappers tottered and tripped, then staggered and fell . . . *splash!* straight into the pool at the deep end. Under the water, glugging and gurgling, they came back up to the surface with a splutter and a cough.

By now Peaches was long gone. Caitlin had sprinted off with her. Megan and Lauren had called Buster, Daisy and Dylan to follow.

Now they were all out of reach of the half-drowned dognappers, running back down the corridor, up the steps and out into the garden, past Henry King's helicopter, across the lawns, out on to Park Road.

"Safe and sound!" Caitlin gasped as another celebrity glided out of Park Central Hotel.

"Thanks to our brave pups!" Lauren beamed.

Buster, Dylan and Daisy looked up at the girls. They wagged their tails. Success for the Puppy Club!

"Now, let's get Peaches back to May Blossom before her dad loses that mega-bucks Galaxy deal!" Megan said, as she strode ahead down the pavement.

CHAPTER ELEVEN

Back at Jerome Towers, May Blossom and Layla were pacing the penthouse floor. A newsflash on TV told them that Henry King was all set to snatch the Galaxy 3 deal.

"This is the worst day of my life," May Blossom groaned as she gazed at her empty Gucci handbag. "Poor little Peaches! Will I ever see her again?"

Will my dad still have a job? Layla wondered. If Rob Jerome lost the Galaxy 3 deal, the answer was a big fat 'No'.

"I don't even know if Peaches is still alive!"

May Blossom wailed. "What if the dognappers, you know, what if—?"

"Don't even think about it!" Layla said quickly.

The two girls stood at the big window and gazed helplessly at the city spread beneath them.

Then the doorbell rang and May Blossom ran to answer it.

She opened the door and Buster bounded in, followed by his owner.

May Blossom stared at Lauren. Megan and Caitlin hung back in the lobby. "Well?" she breathed.

Lauren moved to one side. Caitlin stepped forward. Under her right arm she held Daisy, with her pink ribbon tying up her top-knot. Tucked under her left arm was a little Yorkie wearing a silky yellow ribbon.

"Peaches!" May Blossom cried. She grabbed her puppy and hugged her. She turned round

and round and let
Peaches lick her
tears. "Oh, you've
come home!" she
whispered. "I'm
so happy I'm
crying!"

While Megan,
Lauren, Caitlin
and Layla smiled at
the grand reunion,

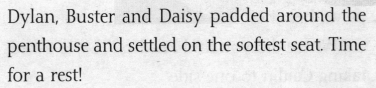

Dylan, Buster and Daisy padded around the
penthouse and settled on the softest seat. Time
for a rest!

"Thank you *so* much!" May Blossom sighed.
"I don't know how you three did this, but
thank you, thank you, thank you!"

"It wasn't us, it was the pups," Caitlin told
her. "They were the ace detectives, tracking
down the dognappers. We just followed."

Dylan, Daisy and Buster sat proudly on the

sofa, their gold Puppy Club medallions dangling from their red ribbons.

"Well, your *puppies* are heroes!" May Blossom told the girls, cuddling her pampered pet to her chest.

"Where did you find Peaches?" Layla asked, taking Caitlin to one side.

"It's a long story," Caitlin began.

Lauren cut in. "Never mind that. We have to call Mr Jerome and tell him we've found Peaches," she insisted loudly.

"We sure do!" May Blossom sprang into action. She put Peaches on the sofa between Daisy and Dylan, then went to call her dad.

Everyone in the room waited on tenterhooks.

"Dad, it's me, May Blossom. We've got Peaches back . . . Yes . . . It was Henry King . . . He kidnapped Peaches. He's a lousy crook. Tell the Galaxy 3 people not to let King sign the deal!"

Lauren nodded. Megan listened carefully. Caitlin held her breath.

May Blossom came off the phone.

"Well?" everyone asked.

There was a long pause. "Too late," May Blossom said, turning down the corners of her mouth.

"Oh no!" Layla cried.

Megan, Lauren and Caitlin all groaned.

"Just kidding!" May Blossom laughed, breaking into a wide grin. "My dad said we left it pretty late, but now he'll be able to blow King's nasty plan sky high!"

"Yippee!" Lauren cried. Megan and Caitlin

did a little dance. Layla sat down and breathed a sigh of relief.

Then May Blossom dug out some doggy treats from her Gucci bag. She gave one each to Buster, Daisy and Dylan. "Good job!" she said, smiling. "You three are a-mazing. To-o-otally cool!"

CHAPTER TWELVE

"The big question," Megan began as the girls and their puppies stepped out on to the pavement outside Jerome Towers, "is how do we get back home?"

Lauren looked up and down the busy street. There was a traffic jam at the red lights. Horns blared, engines chugged. "Maybe we're stuck in Sleuth City forever!" she said, with a deep frown.

For once, Buster sat at her feet and waited patiently.

"Scary!" Megan muttered. She looked down at Dylan, as if hoping he would give her the answer. "I'd rather go home," she added nervously.

Dylan cocked his head and stared back.

"Me too." Caitlin held on to Daisy and gazed up at the tall tower blocks. She glimpsed a patch of blue sky between the buildings. "What if—?" she began.

"What?" Lauren prompted.

"Ssh! Caitlin's thinking," Megan warned.

Caitlin was remembering how this had all started. "We were sitting in your garden, Megan, making our Puppy Club promises . . ."

"So?" Lauren interrupted. "I don't see how that helps."

"Ssh!" Megan said again. "Carry on, Caitlin."

"We put our badges on," Caitlin went on. "Then we gave the pups their medallions."

"Yap!" Daisy gave an encouraging bark.

"Then it all went floaty and weird," Caitlin recalled slowly. "Daisy came to life and we ended up here."

Megan nodded. "I get it!"

"I don't," Lauren sighed.

"So let's do the whole thing the other way round," Caitlin suggested. "See what happens when we take *off* their Puppy Club medallions!"

"Good idea!" Megan nodded again.

"Cool," Lauren agreed.

Daisy, Dylan and Buster pricked up their ears. Their gold medallions hung from the bright red ribbons, glinting in the sun.

"Ready?" Caitlin asked, ready to slip the ribbon over Daisy's head. "All together, one, two, three..."

The tower blocks seemed to tilt and the patch of blue sky spun round. City lights winked and faded.

"It's happening!" Megan cried.

"I'm getting dizzy!" Lauren called out. "Everything's gone blurry. This is so-o-o weird!"

"Are you floating?" Caitlin asked. She looked down at the pavement, at the street lamps and tiny people hurrying by.

A white light surrounded them as they rose higher and higher. It swept them past the tower blocks and up into the clear blue sky, whirling them around and around.

They were back in Megan's garden. The neat lawn sloped down towards the street. Buster scampered after a stray petal blowing across the grass. Dylan sniffed for scents in the hedge bottom.

Lauren gazed at Buster's medallion nestling in the palm of her hand. "That was some adventure!" she gasped.

Megan turned to Caitlin. "Well done for getting us back."

Caitlin nodded. Through the floating and spinning, through the bright light, all the way back from Sleuth City, she'd kept tight hold of Daisy.

Buster and Dylan ran yapping up the lawn. They wagged their tails and jumped up at Lauren and Megan, who were sitting in a heap, trying to make sense of what had just happened.

But Daisy didn't move a muscle. Her brown eyes stared straight ahead. She was a toy dog again.

Caitlin sighed.

"Until next time," Megan said quietly.

"If there *is* a next time," Caitlin murmured.

"There will be," Lauren said with a bright, bright smile. She stood up and reached down to pull her two friends to their feet. "Come on," she said, "Let's say goodbye. Until the Magic Mountain Puppy Club meets again!"

Mystery Pups

This card certifies that

- - - - - - - - - - - - - - - -

is a member of the
Magic Mountain Puppy Club
with his/her puppy

- - - - - - - - - - - - - - - -

Photo
Here

Read more adventures in the

Mystery Pups

series

Three adorable pups. One big mystery!

FRAMED!

The Mystery Pups are back in Sleuth City.
A valuable painting has been stolen and
the wrong person is being blamed. That is
until the Mystery Pups get on the case!

978-1-84738-225-2 £4.99

And coming soon...

 # MISSING!

The feline star of a major movie is missing!
If the Mystery Pups don't find the famous
kitty in time, there's going to be trouble...

978-1-84738-226-9 £4.99